Adventures of Angelina Ballerina

Inspired by the classic children's book series by author
Katharine Holabird and illustrator Helen Craig

Penguin Young Readers
An Imprint of Penguin Random House

PENGUIN YOUNG READERS
Penguin Young Readers Group

Manufactured in China.

ISBN 9781101950173

10 9 8 7 6 5 4 3 2

Table of Contents

Angelina Has the Hiccups!
7

Angelina's Silly Little Sister
37

Angelina and the Flower Garden
67

Angelina at Ballet Camp
97

Angelina Has the Hiccups!

by Katharine Holabird
based on the illustrations by Helen Craig

Penguin Young Readers
An Imprint of Penguin Random House

Angelina loves to dance.

Angelina dances

on the way to school . . .

in the playground . . .

even at bedtime!

Angelina has a very best friend.

Her name is Alice.

Alice loves to dance, too.

Angelina and Alice go
to ballet school every week.

Their teacher is Miss Lilly.

Angelina and Alice

love Miss Lilly.

Today Miss Lilly has a surprise.

"We will give a performance,"

she tells the class.

"The dance is called

The Flower Princesses

and the Dragon."

"Yippee!" everyone shouts.

All the ballet students are

in the show.

Cousin Henry is the dragon.

"ROAR!" Henry roars proudly.

"I am a very scary dragon."

Angelina and the other

mouselings are flower princesses.

Angelina is Rose.

She has a wand with a rose.

Alice is Violet.

Her wand has a violet on top.

Miss Lilly shows her students

the steps in the dance.

The flower princesses twirl and

leap across the room.

Henry the dragon

takes big dragon steps.

Thud! Thud! Thud!

"Practice makes perfect,"

Miss Lilly says.

Every morning, Angelina

gets up early.

"Watch me twirl and leap,"

she says.

"Not in the kitchen!"

Mrs. Mouseling reminds her.

Every day after school,

Angelina and Alice practice.

They know all

the steps by heart.

Today the mouselings try

on their costumes.

"What if I forget the steps?"

says Alice.

Angelina says, "Do not worry.

Just follow me."

Now Alice feels much better.

Henry has his costume, too.

But he will not let anyone see it.

"I want it to be a surprise,"

he says.

On the day of the show,

Angelina is very excited.

Soon Alice arrives.

"Hi," says Alice.

"Hi!" says Angelina.

Then out comes a big—HICCUP!

Hiccup! Hiccup! Hiccup!

Oh no!

Angelina has the hiccups.

"Hold your breath," says Alice.

Angelina holds her breath.

"HICCUP!" she hiccups.

"Try a spoonful of sugar,"

says Mrs. Mouseling.

Angelina eats a spoonful

of sugar.

"HICCUP!" Angelina hiccups.

Then Angelina hiccups all the

way to the theater.

"Blow in a paper bag,"

says Miss Lilly.

Angelina blows in a paper bag.

"HICCUP!" she hiccups.

Angelina puts on her costume.

HICCUP!

Angelina puts on her

ballet slippers.

HICCUP!

Angelina gets her rose wand.

HICCUP!

The music is starting.

"HICCUP!" Angelina hiccups.

Angelina is ready to cry.

How can she be a

hiccuping ballerina?

"ROAR!"

A scary dragon jumps out

at Angelina.

Angelina jumps, too.

But it is only Henry—

Henry the dragon!

"I told Henry to try scaring away

your hiccups," says Alice.

"Did it work?"

Angelina smiles.

No more hiccups!

Onstage, Angelina and Alice
twirl and leap.

The flower princesses turn

the scary dragon into

a friendly dragon.

After the dance,

Angelina hugs Henry.

"Thank you," she says.

"ROAR!" Henry roars proudly.

Angelina's
Silly Little Sister

by Katharine Holabird
based on the illustrations by Helen Craig

Penguin Young Readers
An Imprint of Penguin Random House

This is Angelina's little sister.

Her name is Polly.

Polly follows Angelina everywhere.

This is Angelina's best friend.

Her name is Alice.

Every day they play together

after school.

Angelina and Alice like to dance.

Polly wants to dance, too.

But she can't remember the steps!

Angelina and Alice do cartwheels.

Polly tries to do the same thing.

But she wobbles and falls over!

Today the two mouselings

have a pink tea party.

Polly wants to join.

"Please, I won't spill.

I promise," says Polly.

Ooops! Polly spills the tea

and makes a horrible mess!

Angelina and Alice go inside.

Angelina tells Polly,

"Alice and I want to play

alone now."

"WAAAA!" screams Polly.

Mrs. Mouseling hears Polly.

She gives Polly a hug.

She says to Angelina,

"Please play with Polly

a little longer.

I am making a cheesecake."

Angelina stomps

into the garden with Alice.

Polly skips after them.

"I want to play hide-and-seek,"

Polly tells them.

49

All at once,

Angelina has an idea.

She whispers in Alice's ear.

"Okay, I'll be it,"

Angelina tells Polly.

"Yippee yay!" shouts Polly.

52

Angelina counts to ten:

"One . . . two . . . three . . .

four . . . five . . . six . . .

seven . . . eight . . . nine . . .

TEN!

Ready or not,

here I come!"

Angelina shouts.

Alice is only pretending to hide.

She is behind the garden shed.

"I found you!" Angelina shouts

so Polly can hear.

Angelina points to the apple tree.

"Polly always hides there,"

she whispers.

"Now we can play by ourselves."

Angelina and Alice run
into the house.

They dress up like ballerinas
and dance around the bedroom.

They forget all about Polly.

After a while,

they begin to get hungry.

They smell the cheesecake.

"Let's have our pink tea party

now," suggests Alice.

"First we have to get my sister,"

says Angelina.

Angelina and Alice look

behind the apple tree.

Polly's not there!

"Oh no!" cries Angelina.

"Where has Polly gone?"

Angelina and Alice

search everywhere,

even under the wheelbarrow

and behind the bushes.

Still no Polly!

Angelina is very upset

and runs into the kitchen.

"I lost Polly!" Angelina cries.

"I was not a good big sister.

I didn't want her playing with us."

Mrs. Mouseling gives

Angelina a hug.

"Don't worry," she says kindly.

"Polly fell asleep

under the apple tree.

So I put her to bed."

Angelina races upstairs.

She is so glad to see

her little sister!

"Are you ready for cake?" she asks.

"Yum!" says Polly.

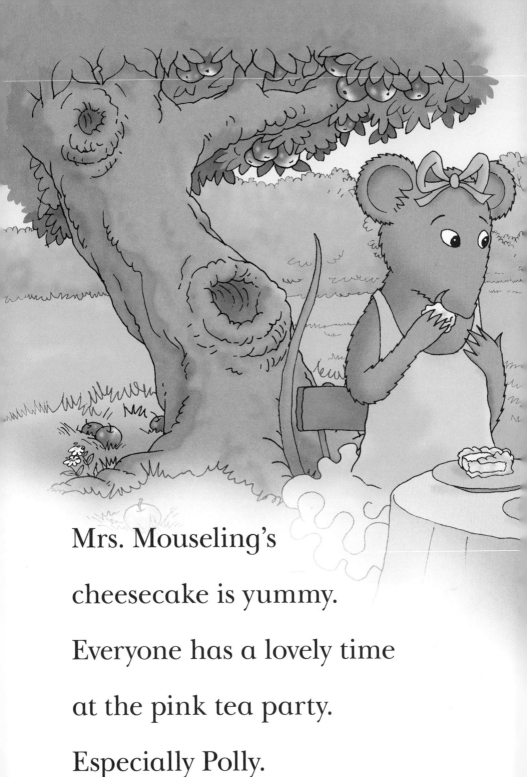

Mrs. Mouseling's

cheesecake is yummy.

Everyone has a lovely time

at the pink tea party.

Especially Polly.

"I will help you pour the tea,"

Angelina says.

"You are a good big sister,"
says Polly.

And this time she spills only
a little bit.

Angelina and the
Flower Garden

by Lana Jacobs
illustrated by Artful Doodlers

Inspired by the classic children's book series by author
Katharine Holabird and illustrator Helen Craig

Penguin Young Readers
An Imprint of Penguin Random House

Angelina is happy.

She loves to be with her friends.

The sun is out.

The birds are singing.

Spring is here!

Angelina has an idea.

"Let's plant a flower garden,"

she says.

Angelina digs a hole.

Alice plants a tiny flower

in the hole.

Polly pats the soil on top.

They all pour water

on the ground.

The mouselings twirl and leap

in their new garden.

Grow, flowers, grow!

Miss Lilly is proud

of the mouselings.

She is proud of their hard work.

It is time to go home.

The mouselings are covered

in dirt and mud.

What a fun day!

At home, Angelina tells her family
about the garden.
"I can't wait to go
back to school tomorrow
to see our garden," she says.

The next day, Angelina goes

to see the garden.

Oh no!

What happened to the flowers?

"The flowers have been trampled,"

says Miss Lilly.

"The birds must have been happy

to see the garden, too," she says.

Angelina is sad.

All their hard work is ruined.

Wait!

Angelina has an idea.

"Why don't we make a garden

for the birds *and* the flowers?"

she says.

What a great idea!

The mouselings get right to work.

Angelina and her friends

build a birdhouse.

Alice *pirouettes* as they hang up

the birdhouse.

Then they gather twigs

to build a nest.

Polly fills up the birdbath.

Now the birds will have

lots of places to rest!

Angelina plants a new batch of
tiny flowers.

"Now the garden is ready

for spring!" says Angelina.

Suddenly a bird flies

into the garden.

He splashes in the birdbath.

Another bird flies

into the birdhouse.

Angelina's plan worked!

It is time to celebrate

with a new spring dance.

Angelina is so happy

to welcome spring

with her friends.

Her old friends—

and her new friends!

Angelina at
Ballet Camp

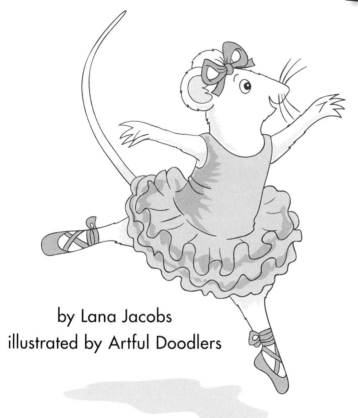

by Lana Jacobs
illustrated by Artful Doodlers

Inspired by the classic children's book series by author
Katharine Holabird and illustrator Helen Craig

Penguin Young Readers
An Imprint of Penguin Random House

Angelina is happy.

The sun is shining.

It is hot outside.

It is summertime!

Angelina is going to ballet
camp this summer.

She wants to dance all day long
at camp.

At her camp, Angelina twirls.

She leaps.

She *pirouettes.*

But something is different about

ballet camp.

Where is Miss Lilly?

Where are Angelina's friends?

Angelina feels sad.

It is time to learn a new dance.

Angelina is having a hard time
learning the steps.
She trips during practice.
Oh no!

That night, Angelina tells her
mom, "I miss school."

"I miss Miss Lilly and all
my friends.
I don't want to go back
to ballet camp!"

Mrs. Mouseling gives Angelina a hug.

"I know it is scary to be in a new place," Mrs. Mouseling tells Angelina.

"But you get to make new friends
and learn new things," she says.
"Doing new things helps you grow.

Don't worry.

Tomorrow will be a better day."

In the morning, Angelina feels

better.

She is ready to go back to ballet

camp.

She smiles at the first mouseling
she sees.

"That is a beautiful dance,"
Angelina says to the mouseling.

"Can you teach me?" Angelina asks.

"Sure!" the mouseling says.

Angelina and her new friend

practice together.

Another mouseling joins in the

dance party.

Now Angelina is having fun!

After lunch, Angelina performs
her new dance routine for her
teacher.

"You worked hard to learn that routine," her teacher says. "I'm so proud of you for not giving up."

Angelina can't wait to show
Alice and Miss Lilly what she has
learned!

Angelina is happy that she stayed at ballet camp.

She made new friends, and she is a better dancer now!

Suddenly, Angelina's best friend,

Alice, walks into the dance

studio.

What a great surprise!

"I'm joining camp, Angelina!"

Alice says.

The two friends hug each other tight.

Angelina can't wait to show Alice
around ballet camp.

They will dance together
every day.

This will be the best summer ever!